This book belongs to

....

....

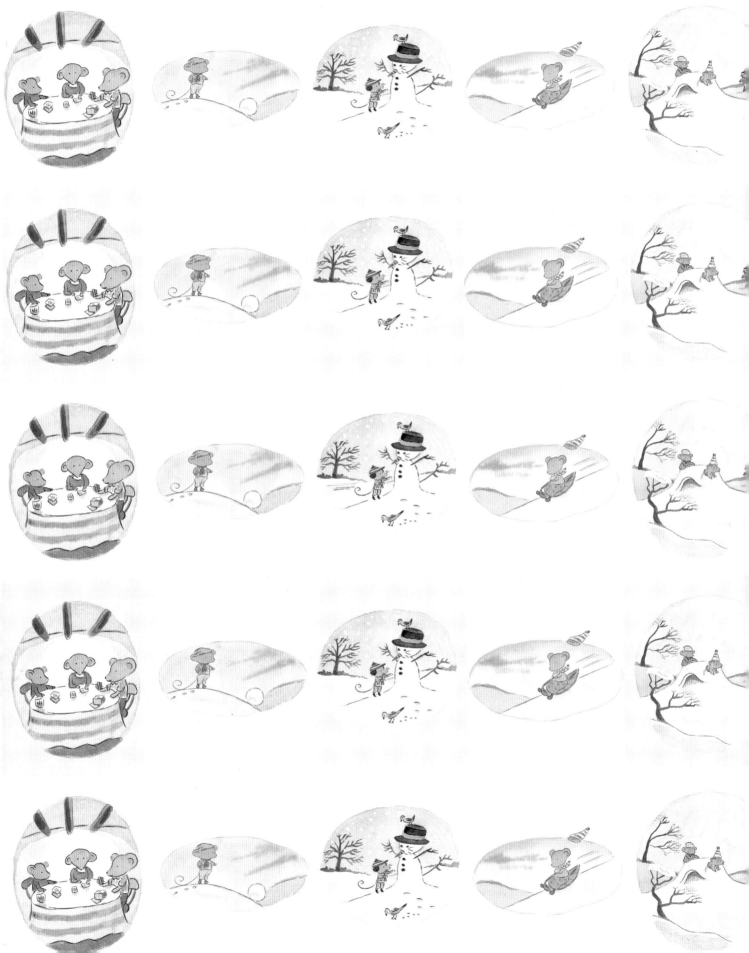

For Carolyn, with love
R.E.

To Brân and Frayla
J.W.

First published in Great Britain in 2006 by Gullane Children's Books
This paperback edition published in 2007 by
Gullane Children's Books
an imprint of Alligator Books
Winchester House, 259-269 Old Marylebone Road,
London NW1 5XJ

1 3 5 7 9 10 8 6 4 2

Text © Richard Edwards 2006
Illustrations © John Wallace 2006

The right of Richard Edwards and John Wallace to be identified
as the author and illustrator of this work has been asserted by them
in accordance with the Copyright, Designs and Patents Act, 1988.

A CIP record for this title is available from the British Library.

ISBN-13: 978-1-86233-703-9

Printed and bound in China

We Love the Snow

Richard Edwards * John Wallace

GULLANE
CHILDREN'S BOOKS

Sadmouse looked up at the sky.
"The snow's coming," he said miserably. "I hate the snow!"
Glummouse looked up at the sky.
"You're right," she said. "The snow's coming. I hate it too!"
Littlemouse looked up at the sky. He was the youngest
of the mice and had never seen the snow before.
"What is the snow?" he asked.
"It's a bad thing." said Sadmouse. "It falls on the world."
"It's a terrible thing." said Glummouse. "It freezes the world."
And they all went back inside.

That night, Littlemouse lay in bed wondering what the thing called snow could be. Was it a sort of ghost that came howling through the trees? Was it a fierce beast, like a fox, only worse? What *was* the snow?

In the morning Littlemouse heard Sadmouse saying
that, as expected, the snow had come in the night.
"It's there now," said Sadmouse. "It's everywhere.
And we can't go outside until it's gone away."

They sat round the table.
"Can I have a peek at the snow to
see what it's like?" Littlemouse asked.
"No, you cannot," said Sadmouse.
"Certainly not!" said Glummouse. "The very idea!"

So they stayed inside because of the snow.
They played mouse-cards. They watched mouse TV.
They talked and they slept.

Then they woke up and played mouse cards
and watched mouse TV some more.

It was boring for Littlemouse. He wanted to see the snow, and find out what it was. It couldn't be that bad! It wasn't banging down their door, or trying to get inside.

So one night, when the others were sleeping, Littlemouse crept out of bed . . .

across the floor . . .

up the stairs . . .

and as quietly as,
well, a mouse,
he opened the door
and went outside
and saw . . .

the snow!

All round the tree it lay, and across
the floor of the wood, and it whitened the bare
branches and gleamed in the moonlight. Littlemouse thought
it was the best thing he had ever seen! He put one paw forward and
touched it. It was cold, but he soon got used to that and went
scurrying over the snow in the quietness of
the midnight wood.

Littlemouse played in the snow.
He made a slide, and found a leaf for a toboggan.

He made a snow ball and pushed it downhill, watching
it get bigger and bigger. He built a snowmouse.

He jumped in the snow.
He rolled in the snow.

And finally with little hops he wrote his name in the snow in
footprints until *Littlemouse* was printed out clearly beneath the moon.

When Littlemouse got back to the mouse hole,
it was almost morning. Quietly he crept inside.
"And where have you been?" said an angry voice. It was Sadmouse.
"I went to see the snow," Littlemouse said.
Sadmouse and Glummouse looked horrified.
"It's *not* a bad thing," Littlemouse told them. "It's cold, but you soon
get used to it, and there are all sorts of things you can do with it."
"Humph! Like what for instance?" asked Glummouse.
"I'll show you!" said Littlemouse.

Grumbling and muttering, the two
other mice followed Littlemouse outside
where the sun was rising over the snow,
making it sparkle and shine.
Littlemouse showed them the
slide he had made...

And the snow mouse . . .
And how to make a snow ball, and Sadmouse
made one and pushed it downhill, watching it
get bigger and bigger.

Then Glummouse sat on a leaf for a toboggan.

And the three mice played together in the snow.

They made snowballs and snow houses and they slid and they jumped.
All morning long the wood rang with mouse squeaks of happiness.
Sadmouse and Glummouse had never laughed so much in all their lives.

Then Littlemouse showed them
how to write in the snow, and soon
their names were printed out.

Sadmouse

Glummouse

"You know, I've never much liked my name," said Sadmouse,
looking at its letters. "I think I'll change it!" He scratched out the
first letter and put in two new ones, making *Gladmouse*.
"Good idea," said Glummouse. "I'll change mine too!"
And she scratched out four letters and put in
three new ones, making *Funmouse*.

Then they played some more before, happy but tired,
Gladmouse, Funmouse and Littlemouse went back home.

They dried their furry bodies in front of the fire.
"Do you think there will be more snow
tonight?" asked Littlemouse.
Gladmouse grinned. "I hope so," he said.
"It's a fine thing, is snow. We love it!"
"We do," said Funmouse.

"Oh, yes!" said Littlemouse. "*We love the snow!*"

Other Gullane Children's Books
for you to enjoy

Brown Bear's Wonderful Secret

Caroline Castle
Tina Macnaughton

Ferdie and the Falling Leaves

Julia Rawlinson
Tiphanie Beeke

Ten in the Bed

Jane Cabrera

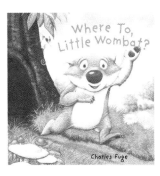

Where To, Little Wombat?

Charles Fuge